THE CALL OF THE WOLVES

by JIM MURPHY ▪ Illustrated by MARK ALAN WEATHERBY

SCHOLASTIC INC./New York

We gratefully acknowledge Wolf Haven America in Tenino, Washington,
for the time and use of their wolves as live models.
And to Jack Laufer, Biologist, Wolf Haven America,
for checking factual details in the text.

Text copyright © 1989 by Jim Murphy
Illustrations copyright © 1989 by Mark Alan Weatherby
Designed by Theresa Fitzgerald
All rights reserved. Published by Scholastic Inc.
SCHOLASTIC HARDCOVER is a registered trademark of Scholastic Inc.

Library of Congress Cataloging-in-Publication Data

Murphy, Jim, 1947–
The call of the wolves / by Jim Murphy;
illustrated by Mark Alan Weatherby.
p. cm.
Bibliography: p.
Summary: A young arctic wolf has a harrowing adventure trying to find
his way back to the pack after being separated from them during a caribou
hunt. Also includes a chapter with general information about wolves.

ISBN 0-590-41941-2
1. Wolves—Juvenile fiction. [1. Wolves—Fiction.]
I. Weatherby, Mark Alan, ill. II. Title.
PZ10.3.M953Cal   1989
[E]—dc19   88-38729
                                                               CIP
                                                                AC

12 11 10 9 8 7 6 5 4 3   0 1 2 3 4/9

Printed in the U.S.A.   36
First Scholastic printing, November 1989

For Lorraine and Jerry Murphy
                              —*J.M.*

To Tony and Val Zamudio
                              —*M.A.W.*

The young wolf sat on a rock, sniffing the raw wind intently. He could pick out the sticky-sweet smell of a spruce tree and the pungent odor of an arctic fox. But the strongest smell was of approaching snow.

Without warning, one of the pups from his pack knocked him from his rock. A second pup joined the playful fighting and nipped at his fur.

The wolf allowed the pups to charge into him. They weighed only forty pounds, much too small to really hurt him. Besides, it was his turn to watch them while their parents rested.

Just then, a piercing howl interrupted their play.

Fifty yards away, the oldest male was pacing nervously. Back and forth he went, back and forth, his body stiff, his ears rammed forward. He stopped to look toward the mountains. Then he raised his head and howled. His mate joined him and their voices blended in an eerie, sad call.

The young wolf saw what was troubling them. The caribou herd, their source of food, was a gray smudge on the horizon. The caribou had also smelled the snow and were moving to a new feeding ground.

The young wolf trotted over to the older wolves. The pups ran after him, yapping and tripping over each other. Another winter had come to the arctic and the wolf pack would follow the caribou.

For eight days, the wolves trailed the caribou. The oldest male and female took turns leading. Both were six years old and knew the easiest routes.

The young wolf was only two and not very experienced at finding trails. He would watch the pups and make sure they did not wander far from the pack.

The terrain grew steeper and more dangerous. Snow began falling. Near the mountain, the pack came to a stream. One at a time, the wolves leaped across.

On the other side, they entered a forest of tall trees. The young wolf could smell food all around, a delicious mix of beaver, berries, mice, and chipmunk.

At last, they came to a long, thin lake. A half mile away, the caribou had gathered in an area filled with trees, plants, and berries. The caribou had found their winter food. The wolves would stay near the caribou.

The pack located a rock overhang where they would be sheltered from the snow. They rested, but at dusk they were up again. The journey had left them with a gnawing hunger. They were eager to hunt.

Down through the snowy woods they glided, heads low to the ground, eyes sparkling, taking in every detail. The powerful odor of the caribou drew them on, directing them. In a few moments the caribou came into view.

The herd had moved to a flat, open space at the tip of the lake. From here, they could see the wolves moving toward them. Quickly the caribou pulled together in a protective circle, the adults on the outside, the young and the sick in the center.

The wolves spread out. Since a healthy caribou could out-run a wolf, the pack had to pick the right animal.

The young wolf circled cautiously. He studied the face of each caribou. It did not take him long to spot a sickly animal.

The other wolves saw the same caribou and moved toward it. At first, the wolves walked slowly. Then they increased their speed to a gentle trot. The next second, the wolves burst into a forty-mile-per-hour sprint.

The entire caribou herd turned to flee, their hooves kicking up large clots of dirt and snow. At the same moment, a plane loaded with illegal hunters zoomed over the treetops.

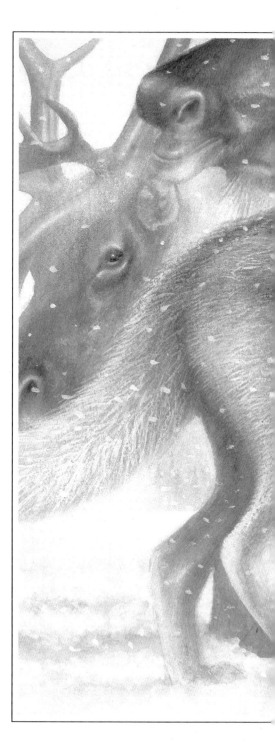

A series of sharp, angry shots rang out from the plane. The noise frightened the caribou and made them charge back at the wolves.

Within moments, the young wolf found himself in a confusion of snorting, frantic animals. He searched for the rest of his pack, but saw only churning legs. To his right, he spotted a sliver of light and headed for the opening.

He broke free of the stampeding caribou only to find the plane coming after him. More shots were fired. He dodged left, then right, his paws a blur as he ran from the lake. But instead of finding safety, the young wolf was running toward a sheer cliff and open sky. Behind him was the plane. He had nowhere to flee to, no other choice. Without hesitating, the wolf launched himself off the cliff.

He sailed into the air, then began dropping. Down, down he fell, his legs still running. A second later, he crashed into a mound of branches and snow.

The impact crumpled his rear leg under him and he yelped in pain. But he couldn't stop. The plane was roaring toward him again.

He tried to run, but each step sent a painful stab up his leg. He shifted his weight so he would run on three legs. His speed increased. Just before the plane reached him, he made it into the protection of the trees.

The wolf kept running through the forest, away from the terrible sound of the plane. Finally, darkness and pain forced him to stop.

He wanted to search for his pack immediately, but he was afraid of the hunters. Instead, he curled up in a tight, warm ball to sleep, alone in the white silence.

At dawn, the wolf shook off the snow that had piled up on him. Then he peered out from under the trees and searched for the hunters. Except for snow, the sky was empty.

Next, he limped into the open and let out a long, lonely howl. There was no answering call. He had to find his pack.

All day the wolf struggled through the snow. It wasn't until late in the afternoon that something moved in the distance. He studied it and was able to make out the ghostly shape of a wolf. A second wolf appeared. Was this his pack?

He was about to approach but didn't. Two other adult wolves had come into view.

The young wolf had trespassed into another pack's territory. And if these wolves saw that he was injured, they would follow him, hoping for an easy kill. He flattened his ears down and scurried away.

The storm grew worse and the wolf had to use his chest to plow through the snow. He was so tired that his breathing became a low, throaty panting.

He turned to see if the wolves were tracking him. At first he saw nothing. Then, far off, the forest came alive with skulking shadows and glowing eyes. He did not wait to rest.

Two hours later, the wolf detected a familiar odor. Food. It was dark and the wolves were somewhere behind him. But it had also been many days since he'd eaten. He moved toward the food.

The food scent led him over a hill. More odors came to him. There was wood smoke, metal, wet fur, and something that reminded him of the hunters. All were troubling and confusing, but he did not stop. Food was too close.

He came around an upended tree. Ahead, he saw a tiny cabin, a spot of light seeping from a door window. Nothing moved or threatened him, but the strange sight made him hesitate. He inched forward, one cautious step at a time, his eyes probing the dark for details. He raised his paw to take another step.

Suddenly, the snow next to him exploded and a sled dog leaped at him, its teeth bared and snapping. Other mounds erupted with angry dogs straining at their chains to get at him. The young wolf sprang from the snarling dogs and fled into the cold night.

Toward morning, the storm lessened and the wolf grew nervous. The other wolves were getting closer. And in the light the hunters might see him. Then he heard rushing water. He'd found the stream.

The rocks were ice-covered and slippery, so the wolf had to creep along to the edge. The water splashed and roared over the rocks, tumbling and churning. Below the falls, the rocks stuck out of the water like jagged black teeth.

The barking of the other pack grew louder. Still, the pain in the young wolf's leg made him pause. A sudden growling behind him forced him to act. He fixed his eyes on the opposite side, tensed his muscles, and jumped.

His foreclaws touched rock and dug in, but his rear legs splashed into the icy water. The water tugged at him and tried to pull him under. His legs fought to hold on. Finally, with one great heave, he pulled himself out of the water.

Behind him, the other wolves had almost reached the water's edge. Soon, they would leap across and be on him.

The young wolf pushed himself up and started to run, only to find the path in front blocked by two wolves. He froze. Had the other wolves circled around to cut off his retreat? All of a sudden, two pups came charging into the open, barking wildly. He'd done it. He had found his way home to his pack!

Before the young wolf could take another step, his pack ran past him and challenged the other pack. When the other wolves saw them, they turned and fled across the snowy landscape.

The young wolf sprinted the short distance to his pack. He slowed to a walk and sniffed to show he was friendly.

But the pups did not wait for the young wolf to greet the adults. They sprang at him in a frenzy of affection, knocking him to the ground and scrambling all over him, licking his face and nipping at his ears.

The oldest male and female raised their heads and howled a greeting. The young wolf and the pups howled, too, their call drifting through the forest, over the hills and snow for many miles.

Every animal who heard the call of the wolves knew that the pack was together again.

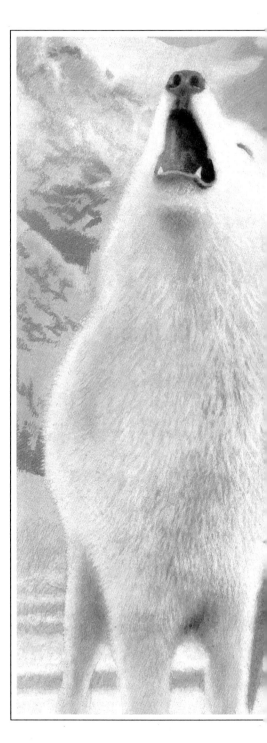

The Wolf—Past, Present, and Future

In the past, people felt wolves were nasty, savage animals that loved to kill wildlife, herd animals, and even humans. This fear and hatred was so strong that people slaughtered hundreds of thousands of wolves. In many regions, cash bounties were even offered to anyone who brought in a dead wolf. By the beginning of this century, wolves were almost completely wiped out in the United States.

Fortunately, the United States government stepped in to protect the last remaining wolves. Wolves were put on the endangered species list and all hunting of them was banned.

In addition, scientists began studying wolves carefully for the first time and were surprised by what they learned. For instance, the idea that wolves hunt humans turned out to be completely false. Wolves are afraid of humans and will run away or hide if they sense a human nearby. In fact, there has never been a documented case of a healthy wolf attacking a human in North America.

Wolves prefer the taste of large game animals, such as moose, caribou, and deer. What's more, they hunt only enough to survive and generally go after a sick or elderly animal. Such selective hunting actually helps keep herds healthy and strong.

Another surprising discovery was that a wolf pack will at times even refrain from hunting altogether. If a caribou herd is very small, wolves will often leave it alone until the caribou have had time to increase in number. Instead, the wolves will turn to other kinds of food, such as rabbit, fox, mice, and even berries. If all food is scarce, a wolf pack will even skip having pups for a year to hold down the demand for food.

Scientists realized that an animal has to be very smart to manage its food supply so carefully. This led to more research—and more surprises.

They discovered that wolves are very social animals. Wolves live in packs of from five to twenty members with two leaders, the alpha male and female. But it is cooperation and shared work that insure a pack's survival. For example, when snow piles up, every adult wolf will take a turn plowing a trail. This makes travel easier for those that follow. Adult wolves share the responsibility of watching over and caring for the pups, and if a member of the pack is unable to hunt, others will bring food back to him or her.

The most startling discovery was the wolf's amazing ability to communicate. One wolf can "talk" to another through the position of his ears, fur, and body, the pitch and intensity of his bark or growl, by nipping at the fur and, of course, through howling. A wolf can communicate more than just anger or fear. Wolves seem to take great joy in the success of a hunt, the small accomplishments of a pup, and even the brilliance of a clear, dark sky filled with stars. And no matter how much time has passed, wolves will recognize and greet a long-absent member of the pack.

It is important to be clear about one thing. Wolves are not meant to be pets. They are very powerful wild animals that need vast amounts of territory in which to roam and hunt. But modern research has shattered the old view of the wolf as a useless, unfeeling creature.

Recently the United States Fish and Wildlife Service began a program to reintroduce wolf packs in areas where they once lived. So far, two small packs have been released in wilderness areas in North Carolina and Florida. Both packs seem to be surviving nicely, so plans are being made to place packs in Montana, Idaho, and Yellowstone National Park in Wyoming. But many people still fear wolves and do not understand their value in nature. And despite the laws, hundreds of wolves are still killed through illegal hunting. It will take many dedicated people and many years before the call of the wolves once again fills the forests of North America.

If You Want to Know More About Wolves

Here is a brief list of very good sources of information about wolves, some with photographs. Your school or public library might be able to help you find them.

Brandenburg, Jim. *White Wolf: Living With an Arctic Legend,* 1988.
Details the life and habits of a pack of white wolves. Spectacular full-color photographs.

Clarkson, Evans. *Wolf Country: A Wilderness Pilgrimage,* 1975.
A first-person account of a journey into an area where wolves thrive.

Lopez, Barry Holstun. *Of Wolves and Men,* 1979.
The best source of information on the physical ability of wolves, their habits, means of communicating, and personality. Includes an extensive discussion of wolf myth and lore.

Mech, David L. *The Wolf: The Ecology and Behavior of an Endangered Species,* 1970.
A straightforward, scholarly examination of wolves and their value in nature.

Mowat, Farley. *Never Cry Wolf,* 1963.
An impassioned and often very funny account of the author's study of wolves in the Canadian wilderness.

Whitaker, John O. *The Audubon Society Field Guide to North American Mammals,* 1980.
A brief, to-the-point summary of wolf information.

In addition to these books, a fine movie version of Farley Mowat's *Never Cry Wolf* is available on video cassette.